Originally published in Spanish in 2020 as *Los carpinchos* by Ediciones Ekaré
Text and illustrations copyright © 2019 by Alfredo Soderguit
English translation copyright © 2021 by Elisa Amado
First published in Canada, the U.S. and the U.K. by Greystone Books in 2021

21 22 23 24 25 6 5 4 3 2

Greystone Kids / Greystone Books Ltd.
greystonebooks.com

An Aldana Libros book

Cataloguing data available from Library and Archives Canada
ISBN 978-1-77164-782-3 (cloth)
ISBN 978-1-77164-783-0 (epub)

Editing by Carmen Diana Dearden
Copyediting by Dawn Loewen
Proofreading by Elizabeth McLean
Jacket and text design by Alejandra Varela

Printed and bound in China by 1010 Printing International Ltd.

Greystone Books gratefully acknowledges the Musqueam, Squamish, and Tsleil-Waututh peoples on whose land our office is located.

Greystone Books thanks the Canada Council for the Arts, the British Columbia Arts Council, the Province of British Columbia through the Book Publishing Tax Credit, and the Government of Canada for supporting our publishing activities.

THE CAPYBARAS

Alfredo Soderguit

TRANSLATED BY Elisa Amado

AN ALDANA LIBROS BOOK

GREYSTONE KIDS

GREYSTONE BOOKS • VANCOUVER/BERKELEY

That was a safe, agreeable place.

Life was comfortable and everyone knew
what she was supposed to do.

There was plenty of food,
and nothing out of the ordinary ever happened.

Until one day

the capybaras came.

No one knew them,

no one expected them.

There were lots of them,
they were hairy,
they were wet,
they were too big.

NO!

There was no room for them.

But the capybaras couldn't
go home

because hunting season
had begun.

To be allowed to stay,
the capybaras had to accept
some rules:

1. Don't make any noise.

2. Don't come out of the water.

3. Don't come near the food.

4. Don't question the rules.

The rules were for everyone.
No one had permission
to go near the capybaras.

They were wild animals,

and they might be dangerous.

Then everything changed.

The days changed.

And so did the nights.

Hunting season ended.

The capybaras expressed their gratitude
for being given refuge
and got ready to leave.

That year's hunt
hadn't gone well.

The hunters returned
empty handed.

The chicken coop
was empty too.

No one ever knew
what had happened.